FIREMAN SAM
AND THE FARM FIRE

story by Caroline Hill-Trevor
illustrations by The County Studio

Developed from a storyline by Rob Lee
and a script by Nia Ceidiog

GUILD PUBLISHING

LONDON · NEW YORK · SYDNEY · TORONTO

It was a very hot afternoon and Jupiter was returning to Pontypandy after the third fire that day.

"Well, I certainly hope that was the last fire for a while," said Fireman Sam. "It's too hot to be putting out fires – We'd be better off at the seaside."

"You're right, Sam," replied Station Officer Steele, wiping his face with a big red hanky. "But blazing hot weather like this means a lot of fires. Isn't that right Cridlington?"

"Sarah and James look as if they'd rather be at the seaside too," said Elvis as they pulled up beside Bella's potato patch.

"Hello there you two," said Fireman Sam. "Picking potatoes... Not exactly the weather for chips, is it? Maybe Bella's making some of her special potato salad," he said hopefully.

"No, Uncle Sam, it's for ice cream," answered Sarah, looking hot and bothered.

"Um," said Elvis looking puzzled, "I've never heard of potato ice cream – it must be new."

"Oh Elvis, Bella is going to give us some ice cream if we fill the buckets with potatoes for her – not make ice cream out of them!" said James impatiently. "Come on Sarah, the harder we work, the sooner we'll be finished."

"Rightio, we'd best be getting back as well. Keep up the good work Sarah!" said Fireman Sam, looking thoughtful.

When Jupiter had driven out of sight Sarah and James
stopped for a break and noticed a wisp of smoke billowing
from the hillock overlooking the potato patch.

"There can't be another fire," cried Sarah.

"It could be coming from a barbecue I s'pose," said James.
"Come on – it's safest to check anyway."

They ran up the hill.

"Oh no! It's the barn at Pandy Lane Farm. What about the animals?" shouted James. "There's a call box down the road – we must get Jupiter out quickly."

Breathlessly Sarah dialled 999 and asked for the Fire Service.

Jupiter was back at the Fire Station. The crew had just
sat down with a cup of tea when the alarm went off.
Fireman Sam tore the details off the printer.

"Fire at the barn at Pandy Lane Farm," he read out.
"Right, let's get going."

Fireman Sam, Station Officer Steele and Elvis slid down
the pole and leapt into the cab without wasting a second.

For the fourth time that day Jupiter set out with the siren wailing.

"Mama Mia, another fire" said Bella, watching Jupiter rush through the village.

"Looks serious. Where's my Norman got to now?" said Dilys Price, looking around nervously. "He set out with a picnic and his fishing rod hours ago. I hope he's not in any trouble."

As the Firemen approached Pandy Lane Farm, they met Trevor driving his bus back towards Pontypandy.

"Turn around and follow us, Auxiliary Fireman Trevor Evans," commanded Station Officer Steele. "We're going to need all the help we can get. Speed up Cridlington, never mind the bumps," he ordered as they turned down the track leading to the farm.

Together Elvis and Fireman Sam manned the hose and the water gushed out – WHOOSH!

"Oh no," remembered Fireman Sam, "we didn't check the water level in Jupiter's tank. Let's hope we've got enough. We must stop this fire spreading."

"Come on Trevor – you've a way with animals, we must move them," said Station Officer Steele, as a frightened hen zoomed overhead squawking. "Get the cows and the donkey out, and don't forget the ducks."

"I hope this isn't the stubborn kind of donkey," muttered Trevor as he tied a rope round its neck. It wasn't. The next moment Trevor found himself flying out of the barn in a flurry of feathers as the geese also made their escape, honking angrily.

Trevor chased out all the cows and ducks, but just as he and Station Officer Steele were congratulating themselves, Sarah and James pointed at the barn roof.

 "Look up there Trevor – some hens are trapped in the rafters – they'll get burnt," shouted Sarah.

 "Don't you worry Sarah, we'll save them," said Station Officer Steele. "We'll get the ladder out. Fireman Evans is going up."

Trevor quickly climbed the ladder and shooed the hens out, waving one arm and holding on tightly with the other hand. "Good with animals I may be," he thought to himself, "but these hens are giving me vertigo."

But just as all the animals were out of the barn and the fire
was finally under control the hose started to splutter.
Instead of whooshing out the water slowed to a trickle.

"What shall we do now?" said Elvis. "We still have to damp
everything down. I know! Find a hydrant."

"No hydrants out here in the wilds, Elvis," pointed out
Fireman Sam.

"Well, a drain'll have to do then," said Elvis, thinking quickly.

"Good thinking Cridlington," said Station Officer Steele, looking relieved.

"Uh, Sir, there are no drains out here either," said Fireman Sam, "but there is a pond down the road – let's get down there double quick, before the fire flares up again."

They jumped into Jupiter and drove off down the road to fill up the tank with pond water. When they left the pond was almost empty.

Norman Price had been fishing quietly by the pond all afternoon and had fallen asleep after his picnic.

"Oh no, now what've I done?" he said, waking up to see the pond emptying. "Beginner's luck – I can't catch a fish but I have caught the plug, and pulled it out, by the look of things. Better get out of here before anyone comes." And he hurried off towards Pandy Lane Farm.

Back at the farm the crew damped down the fire with the pondwater.

"You were all terrific," said James.

"What a good job you remembered that pond, Uncle Sam," said Sarah. "It's lucky no fish live in it!"

"Shoo, shoo, shoo. Get out of my bus, you ungrateful birds.
Fine thanks for rescuing you, this is, Ssss! Ssss!" said
Trevor, running at the hens with both arms waving.

"Whatever's all that noise," said Fireman Sam, turning
round to see. "Oh look, Trevor Evans and his amazing
travelling chicken run. Poor Trevor!"

Norman came up. "What's been going on? Have I missed the excitement?"

"Hello Norman, been fishing – did you catch anything?"

Norman went bright red. "Only the plug. I fell asleep and now the pond's empty – I must've pulled it out."

"Well I wouldn't worry about it, if I were you, Norman," said Fireman Sam, winking at Sarah and James. "We used the water to damp down this fire. Now let's see about Bella's potatoes. Can I borrow your fishing rod please Norman?" He led the way back to the pond.

Using Norman's fishing rod Fireman Sam pulled a bicycle and an old pram out of the pond and made them into a very strange contraption. Sarah looked puzzled.

"Brill, Uncle Sam, but ... what is it?"

"Let me demonstrate the Samuel Patent Potato Picker," Fireman Sam said proudly. He pushed it up the field and quickly filled the buckets.

"Thanks Uncle Sam, that's great," said Sarah and James together.

"O Bellissima, now I know who the best potato pickers are;
thank you, thank you," said Bella when she saw all the
potatoes.

"Uncle Sam helped us," said Sarah.

"Yes, but you helped us too," said Station Officer Steele.

"Then you all deserve my best Italian ice cream.

FIREMAN SAM SAYS

Hot, dry weather can mean lots of fires in forests and dry grassland. When you're in the countryside be especially careful not to do anything that might cause a fire. Take all your litter home, especially glass bottles.

This edition published 1989 by
Guild Publishing
by arrangement with William Heinemann

First published 1989 by William Heinemann
Fireman Sam © 1985 Prism Art & Design Ltd
Text © 1989 William Heinemann Ltd
All rights reserved

Based on the animation series produced by Bumper Films
for S4C – Channel 4 Wales – and Prism Art & Design Ltd

Original idea by Dave Gingell and Dave Jones, assisted
by Mike Young

Characters created by Rob Lee

Printed in Great Britain by
Springbourne Press Ltd
CN 5156